SHAKER LANE

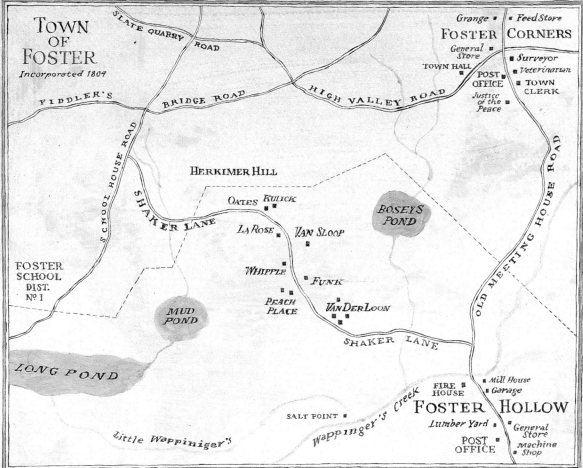

ALICE AND MARTIN PROVENSEN

VIKING KESTREL

E
C.3

To Karen and Kelly

VIKING KESTREL

Viking Penguin Inc., 40 West 23rd Street, New York, New York 10010, U.S.A.
Penguin Books Ltd, 27 Wrights Lane, London W8 5TZ (Publishing & Editorial) and
Harmondsworth, Middlesex, England (Distribution & Warehouse)
Penguin Books Australia Ltd, Ringwood, Victoria, Australia
Penguin Books Canada Limited, 2801 John Street, Markham, Ontario, Canada L3R 1B4
Penguin Books (N.Z.) Ltd, 182–190 Wairau Road, Auckland 10, New Zealand

First published in 1987 by Viking Penguin Inc.
Published simultaneously in Canada

Printed in Japan by Dai Nippon Printing Co. Ltd.
Set in Garamond #3

1   2   3   4   5   91   90   89   88   87

Library of Congress Cataloging in Publication Data
Provensen, Alice.   Shaker lane.
Summary: When the town decides to build a reservoir on their land, the residents of Shaker Lane
decide to move away rather than fight to keep their homes.
[1. City and town life—Fiction.   2. Moving, Household—Fiction]   I. Provensen, Martin.
II. Title.   PZ7.P9457Sh   1987   [E]   87-6283   ISBN 0-670-81568-3

OT SO LONG AGO, if you went down School House Road and crossed Fiddler's Bridge, you would come to Shaker Lane. A Shaker Meeting House once stood at the crossroads. Nothing was left of it but a few stones.

Scrub brush covered the old farmland on both sides of the road.
The farm belonged to the Herkimer sisters, Abigail and Priscilla.

They were old ladies. They sat all day in their front yard facing the road.
No one mowed their fields. No one fixed the fences.

In order to live, the Herkimer sisters sold off pieces of the farm,
a half-acre here, an acre there.

They sold it cheap.
In a year or two there was a row of houses along Shaker Lane.

In the first house along the road lived Virgil Oates with his wife, Sue Ann,
their five kids, and Sue Ann's brother, Wayne.
Next to it was Sam Kulick's place.

Across the road lived Norbert La Rose. His wife's name was Charlene.
They had four kids.
They also had three dogs, five cats, and a duck named Lucy.

The people who lived on Shaker Lane
took things easy.
Their yards were full of stuff—
old dressers waiting to go inside,
cars that would never roll again,
parts of old trucks,
stovepipes, piles of rotten rope, rusty tin,
bedsprings, bales of old wire and tin cans.
Some people would have liked to see
Shaker Lane disappear forever.

When the big yellow school bus came down
Shaker Lane, the kids would yell,
"Aker, baker, poorhouse shaker!"

Sometimes there were fights.

Here is Old Man Van Sloop's house.
Dozens of dogs lived here, as well as
chickens and a goat named Shem.
The dogs came and went just as they felt like.
They fought and slept and chewed
on the bones
that Old Man Van Sloop found
for them somewhere.

Sometimes an angry man showed up,
looking for a runaway.
Old Man Van Sloop didn't care.
"Plenty more where that one came from!"
he would shout.

The man would frown and say,
"Public nuisance!" and take his dog away.

Next to Old Man Van Sloop lived the Whipple boys, Jesse and Ben.
They were twins and did yard work.
People never knew if it was Jesse or Ben who weeded their gardens.

Back of the Whipple house was the Peach place. Bobbie Lee Peach and his wife, Violet,
lived here with their children—Emma, Zekiel, Sophie, Harvey, and Ralph.
Violet's father, Chester Funk, lived with them too.

Here is Big Jake Van der Loon.
Big Jake could do anything.
He had four helpers: Little Jake,
Herman, Matty, and Buddy.
Big Jake dug wells, moved barns,
put up fences.

He put up a telephone pole
for the Herkimer sisters.
He moved a chicken coop for Sam Kulick.
When an enormous maple tree blew down
in a storm, Big Jake cut up firewood
for everyone.

The Van der Loon family lived in four houses on Shaker Lane.
One for Big Jake, one for his brother-in-law, Harold Prideux; one for LeRoy
and Milly Cobb; and one for Big Jake's mother, Big Ethel.

One day Ben Whipple came running up to Big Ethel.
"We're going to be flooded out!" he shouted.
"They're building a dam on Bosey's Pond!"

It was true.

Ed Rikert, the County Land Agent,

came to Shaker Lane.

"A reservoir is to be built," he said.

"Most of you folks will have to move.

The county will pay you for your land."

STATE SUPREME COURT
COUNTY OF FOSTER

NOTICE OF PETITION TO ACQUIRE REAL PROPERTY PURSUANT TO THE EMINENT DOMAIN PROCEDURE LAW

In the Matter of the Eminent Domain
Procedure Law Proceeding by the

TOWN OF FOSTER,
                        Petitioner,

- Against -

Virgil Oates,
                        Respondent,

INDEX NO.
12580 914
GRID # 03
6367-00-
681397-00

PLEASE TAKE NOTICE, that the petition for acquisition of real property and the filing of an acquisition map pursuant to the Eminent Domain Procedure Law of the **COUNTY OF FOSTER** in the above entitled proceeding, will be presented to the State Supreme Court at a Term thereof to be held in and for the Town of Foster, at the Foster County Courthouse, on twelfth day of October, in the forenoon of said day, and a motion will then and there be made that said petition be granted and that an Order be issued vesting title to the real property described in the petitioner.

FOSTER COUNTY DEPT. OF PUBLIC WORKS	
LAND TO BE ACQUIRED FROM:	Virgil Oates.
FOR:	Construction of Dam and Reservoir.
TOWN:	Foster.
VALUATION:	To be determined.

Edward N. Beuler

Edward N. Beuler,
Foster County Attorney.

COUNTY OFFICE BUILDING
222 EAST MARKET STREET.

Virgil Oates was the first to leave.
"Can't swim," he said.
Then the Whipple boys and
the Peaches packed up and left.
One by one,
the other families followed.

The bulldozers came. Huge painted monsters, like iron dinosaurs, chewed up Shaker Lane.

Until, at last, the excavation was complete.

The water rose slowly but surely. It crept over the last chimney.

Only the Herkimer house was still there, high on the hill.

What was left of Shaker Lane changed its name to Reservoir Road.

You wouldn't know the place.

Old Man Van Sloop is still here.
He has a houseboat.
He has his chickens
and Shem, the goat.

Lots of dogs still come to visit.

"I like the water," says Old Man Van Sloop.